Naughty Fairies

maya

Caterpillar Thriller

maya

Collect all the Naughty Fairies books:

Caterpillar Thriller

Lucy Mayflower

Hodder
Children's
Books

a division of Hachette Children's Books

Special thanks to Lucy Courtenay

Created by Hodder Children's Books and Lucy Courtenay
Text and illustrations copyright © 2006 Hodder Children's Books
Illustrations created by Artful Doodlers

First published in Great Britain in 2006
by Hodder Children's Books

4

A Catalogue record for this book is available from the British Library

ISBN – 10: 0 340 91179 4
ISBN – 13: 978 0 340 91179 2

Printed and bound in Great Britain
by Bookmarque Ltd, Croydon, Surrey

The paper and board used in this paperback by Hodder Children's Books
are natural recyclable products made from wood grown in
sustainable forests. The manufacturing processes conform to the
environmental regulations of the country of origin.

Hodder Children's Books
A division of Hachette Children's Books
338 Euston Rd, London NW1 3BH

Contents

Ambrosia Academy

WOOD STUMP

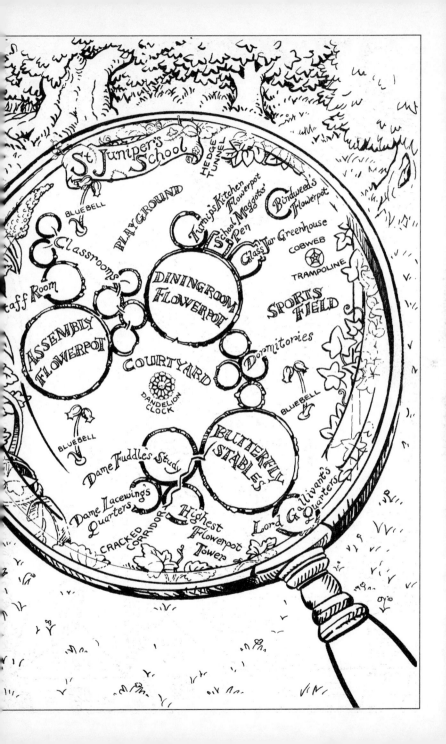

1

Green-Eyed Sprout

Down at the bottom of the garden, dawn was creeping over the hedge. Six fairies were pulling hard on a long piece of grass, trying to bend it down to the ground.

Well, five of them were pulling. The other one was shouting instructions.

"Harder!" Brilliance called. "You'll never get it down like that."

The long piece of grass bent a little closer to the ground.

"Easy for you to say," puffed the fairy at the front. "You're not pulling."

"I'm organising, Tiptoe," said Brilliance patiently. "I can't pull *and* organise."

"I thought you could do anything, Brilliance," said a pretty, spiky-haired fairy at the base of the grass stalk.

The blonde, short-haired fairy in the middle started laughing. Two tiny spiders dangled from her ears like earrings.

"Shut up, Ping," Brilliance scowled. "And you can stop laughing, Nettle."

The grass stalk creaked and groaned. Its feathery head was almost touching a small green hummock, which stood a little higher than the rest of the field.

"Now what?" panted a dark-eyed fairy. A large green caterpillar was draped around her shoulders like a scarf.

"Let go," said a cross-looking fairy in a yellow and black bumblewool jumper dress. "Preferably when you're holding on, Brilliance, and the rest of us aren't."

"We're *not* letting go, Kelpie," said Brilliance. "In answer to your question,

Sesame, we now attach the grass head to the ground. Nettle, can we have some spider silk?"

Brilliance lifted Nettle's ear spiders off her ears and put them on a nearby leaf. As soon as the spiders had spun enough silk, Brilliance plaited it into a stout rope.

The grass stalk shivered. The fairies redoubled their hold on its thick, springy stem.

"Hurry up!" Tiptoe squeaked.

Brilliance looped the silk rope around the grass head. She took two sharp-looking rose thorns from her pocket and whacked them into the little hummock. Then she tied the ends of the silk rope to the thorns and stood back. "OK," she said. "Let go."

The grass stalk bucked and wriggled, but stayed where it was. Everyone cheered.

"Brilliant," said Brilliance with

satisfaction. She tied an extra length of spider silk to one of the thorns, and unravelled it as far as the hedge. Then she scattered some clover leaves over the grass stalk until it was hidden from view. "There," she said. "If that doesn't liven up this morning's lesson, nothing will."

"Is it time for breakfast yet?" said Tiptoe hopefully. "I'm starving."

"I want to check on Pong," said Ping.

"You checked on your precious dragonfly when we came out," said Kelpie. "It's stupid to check him again."

"I'll check him if I want," Ping snapped.

Nettle glanced at a nearby dandelion clock, growing in a patch by the Hedge. "It's almost half past the dandelion," she said. "We'd better hurry back to our dormitory, or Dame Lacewing will notice we aren't there when she calls us for breakfast."

"I'm going to check on Pong first," said Ping stubbornly.

As Ping and Kelpie argued, Sesame started following the others towards the flowerpot towers of St Juniper's. But halfway along the path, she stopped. A ladybird was struggling feebly in the long grass. It lay on its back and waved its legs at her.

"Poor thing!" Sesame gasped. She put Sprout on the ground and bent down to take a closer look. Sprout squeaked jealously.

"Come on, Sesame!" Brilliance called. "We'll be late!"

As gently as she could, Sesame tipped the ladybird over, so that its legs were touching the ground. It had beautiful shiny black spots on its berry-red back. One of its wing cases was crumpled, and it was having trouble walking.

"This ladybird needs our help!" Sesame said. Sprout gave something close to a growl. "We have to take it back to school so I can look after it!"

Kelpie stopped arguing with Ping. "I'm not getting all soppy over a ladybird," she said in disgust.

"Please, Kelpie!" said Sesame, biting her lip. "Imagine if it was Flea that was sick."

"My bumblebee never gets sick," said Kelpie. She looked a little softer.

"You English fairies!" said Ping

scornfully. "No one bothers with ladybirds in China."

"You've never been to China," Brilliance pointed out.

Ping looked thunderous.

Sesame stroked the ladybird's head. "I'll look after it," she said. Sprout growled a little louder. "The rest of you won't have to do anything," she added. "It's just – I can't carry it back to school on my own."

"The rest of us can take the ladybird inside while you check on Pong, Ping," Tiptoe suggested.

"I was going to check on Pong anyway," Ping said. And she whirred her lilac wings and flew towards the Butterfly Stables.

Nettle, Brilliance, Tiptoe and Kelpie lifted the ladybird up. "Careful," said Sesame anxiously. "We don't want to dent his other wing."

Sprout growled more loudly.

"Cheer up, Sprout," said Kelpie. "At least it's not another caterpillar."

Twenty dandelion seeds later, the ladybird was safely on Sesame's bed with an acorn cup of water and a bandage on its leg. Brilliance, Nettle, Ping, Kelpie, Tiptoe and Sesame stood in the breakfast queue in the Dining Flowerpot, along with the other pupils

at St Juniper's, the famous fairy school.
A hairy, hungry-looking bumblebee
hovered close above Kelpie's head.
Curled up in Sesame's arms, Sprout
was making a wailing noise.

"Why did you say that about another
caterpillar, Kelpie?" Sesame demanded,
as they shuffled up the queue. "It's
really upset Sprout."

Kelpie shrugged. "Sprout shouldn't
be so sensitive," she said. "There's
hardly any other caterpillars around at
the moment anyway. They're all turning
into butterflies."

"When's Sprout going to turn into a
butterfly?" Nettle asked, helping herself
to a bowl of steaming pumpkin-seed
porridge.

"Soon, I expect," said Sesame,
nuzzling Sprout with her nose.

"I saw the butterfly riding teacher,
Lord Gallivant, at the stables when I
was checking on Pong," said Ping. "He

told me about the Butterfly Cup."

Sesame looked astonished. "You didn't know about it?" she said. She couldn't imagine not knowing about the Butterfly Cup.

Ping shrugged. "This is my first year at St Juniper's, remember? He won't let me enter Pong," she added indignantly.

"Of course he won't," Brilliance said. "Pong's a dragonfly."

"And he's not going to turn into a butterfly any time in the next two weeks," said Tiptoe.

"*Four* weeks," Sesame corrected.

"Nope," said Tiptoe, pouring out a cup of elderflower juice. "Two. They brought it forward. The butterflies are hatching early this year. Dame Fuddle announced it in assembly yesterday. Weren't you listening?"

"No, Sesame and I were too busy putting an aphid down Brilliance's neck," Kelpie said. She took a pile of

honeycakes. The bumblebee flying
around her head buzzed with
excitement. "Shut up, Flea," she said.
"You'll get your food in a minute."

"But . . . I'm on the St Juniper's team
for the Butterfly Cup!" Sesame said in
horror. She tugged Sprout from around
her neck and stared at him. Sprout

stared back nervously. "I'm supposed to ride Sprout! It'll take him at least two weeks to turn into a butterfly, and he's not showing any signs of starting!"

"You can still ride him," said Kelpie.

"I can?" said Sesame hopefully.

"Sure," said Kelpie. "You just won't win. Caterpillars can't fly, see. It's a bit of a disadvantage in a butterfly race." She tossed a honeycake in the air. "Here, Flea – catch!"

2
Fairy Sports

The Butterfly Cup was the biggest
sporting event of the year. St Juniper's
competed against another local fairy
school, Ambrosia Academy. Ambrosia
Academy always won, but this didn't
stop St Juniper's from going butterfly
crazy. Everyone talked about wing
speed and different types of butterfly
powder. Everyone gossiped about
grooming and flying techniques. Most
of all, everyone talked about how
everything would be different this year,
and St Juniper's would win.

It seemed to Sesame that suddenly
the whole Dining Flowerpot was talking
about the Butterfly Cup.

". . . past his prime now, but he came close last year . . ."

". . . added ground violets to his butterfly powder, which made him smell nice but he was still rubbish . . ."

". . . crashed straight into the Wood Stump . . ."

"What am I going to *do?*" Sesame said for the hundredth time, as they walked to the Sports Field for their first lesson. Sprout hung meekly around her neck.

"Talk to Lord Gallivant," suggested Brilliance.

"He'll just go on about how he won the Midsummer Champion Butterfly Race and how I shouldn't let a little thing like not having a butterfly get me down," Sesame said in despair. The Midsummer Champion Butterfly Race was Lord Gallivant's favourite subject.

"Who else is riding for St Juniper's?" Tiptoe asked.

"Onion, Vetch, and Pelly," said Brilliance, ticking them off on her fingers one by one.

"Onion and Vetch?" said Kelpie in disgust. "They can't ride to save their lives. Their butterflies are practically dead."

"Who's Pelly?" Ping said.

"Her real name is Pelargonium," said Tiptoe. "But if you call her that, she hits you."

"Could be a problem in the middle of the race," said Kelpie, as they arrived at the Fairy Sports Field.

"Sprout might still hatch into a butterfly in time," Tiptoe said. "And if he doesn't, you can borrow a school butterfly. You're a good rider, Sesame," she added loyally. "You could win a race on a twig."

"The school butterflies are worse than twigs," Kelpie sniffed, "especially snowball."

Sesame covered her face with her
hands. Sprout pushed at her fingers.

"Cheer up," Brilliance said. "Dame
Taffeta's coming."

Sesame lifted her face to see Dame
Taffeta, Fairy Science teacher and
reluctant Fairy Sports instructor, flying
gently towards them over the flowerpot
towers of St Juniper's.

Brilliance grinned. "Action stations," she murmured.

The fairies hurried over to the fence. Brilliance checked the trap one last time and gave the hidden silk rope a gentle tug. On the little grass hummock in the middle of the field, the scattered clover leaves shivered.

"Seems a shame," said Kelpie, as Dame Taffeta came in to land on the

hummock with a whirr of wings. "Dame Taffeta always gives tests when she gets annoyed. I prefer doing sports."

Dame Taffeta touched down.

"So do I," said Brilliance.

She pulled the hidden silk rope. On the little hummock, the rose thorns pinged out of the ground.

"Wha . . . wheee!" Dame Taffeta shot into the air as the grass stalk snapped upright.

All the fairies stopped gossiping about the Butterfly Cup and stared.

"I can see Dame Taffeta's pants," said Tiptoe conversationally.

"Whooo!" Dame Taffeta cartwheeled through the sky and landed head first on the cobweb trampoline.

"Couldn't have planned it better myself," said Nettle, looking impressed as Dame Taffeta bounced off the cobweb trampoline and landed halfway up the ivy-covered fence.

Sesame shaded her eyes and looked
up at the fence. "Are you all right,
Dame Taffeta?" she asked.

"Did you trip?" asked Ping.

Dame Taffeta's ears had gone a kind
of dark purple.

"INSIDE!" she roared. "TEST! NOW!"

"I'm in so much trouble," said Sesame
gloomily, as they handed in their test
papers and filed out of the Fairy
Science flowerpot. "I don't have a
butterfly for the Butterfly Cup, and I

didn't write a thing in that test. What
else can go wrong today?"

"Maybe that ladybird's dead," Kelpie
suggested.

"The ladybird! I'd forgotten all about
it!" Sesame gasped. "It's bound to be
dead, and it's all my fault!"

Inching beside Sesame, Sprout gave a
satisfied squeak.

Suddenly, all Sesame's problems
rushed in on her like a wave. "Don't
talk to me, Sprout," she shouted
furiously. "You're a rubbish caterpillar.

You could be a runner bean, for all the use you are. Go away!"

Sprout blinked. The fairies all stared at Sesame in astonishment. They'd never heard her explode like that.

Sesame shook her hair angrily over her shoulders. "I have to go and check on the ladybird. Tell Dame Fuddle I'll be a bit late for Fairy Deportment." And

she spread her wings and zoomed up to the dormitory window.

Inside the dormitory, the ladybird was asleep. Sesame polished its wing cases gently, and worked at the dented part with her fingers to smooth it all out. She tried not to think about the look on Sprout's face when she had shouted at him.

The ladybird stirred. Sesame stroked its glossy black and white head. Tears started in her eyes. If she couldn't ride a decent butterfly in the Butterfly Cup, she'd *die*.

"Think, Sesame," she told herself fiercely. "There's still two weeks to go. Maybe I can catch one in the meadow, or shave a moth and pretend it's a butterfly, or . . ."

Dame Fuddle's voice floated up to the dormitory window. "A one, TWO . . . a one, TWO . . . Heads up, fairies! You look like rhubarb in a rainstorm!"

Sesame looked out of the window at the Fairy Deportment class. The fairies were trying to balance along a line of daisy petals neatly laid out in the courtyard. Dame Fuddle, Head of St Juniper's, was tapping her wand in the palm of her hand with a *one two, one two* beat. Little sparks of light jumped from the tip of the wand.

"Never look at your feet!" Dame Fuddle said. "A fairy always looks ahead! A one, TWO . . . a one, TWO!"

Sesame flew out of the dormitory window and landed lightly on the daisy petals between Tiptoe and Kelpie. She looked around for Sprout.

"Don't move the petals now!" Dame Fuddle shouted. "You look like a lurching trout, Kelpie! Lift your feet!"

Dame Fuddle often spoke in exclamation marks.

"Trout don't have feet, Dame Fuddle," Kelpie said.

"They do in China," said Ping, from somewhere at the back of the line.

"You've never been to China," Brilliance and Nettle said together, from somewhere at the front.

The fairies began to giggle. The line of daisy petals was starting to look a bit ragged.

"Where's Sprout, Tiptoe?" Sesame whispered, trying to point her toes and walk in time with Dame Fuddle's beat.

"Gone," said Tiptoe. She flapped her wings a little, to keep her balance.

"Gone?" Sesame stared at her. "Gone where exactly?"

"Away," Tiptoe said. "Like you told him to."

"I wish Flea would do what I told him to," Kelpie said.

Sesame forgot about the petals. She stopped pointing her toes. She stopped moving all together. "But I didn't *mean* for him to go away!" she stuttered.

Kelpie stopped as well. "Too bad Sprout didn't know that. Whoops," she added cheerfully, as the line of fairies behind her crashed into each other.

3

Spying

Sesame couldn't concentrate for the rest of the lesson. She kept thinking about how horrible she'd been to Sprout. She'd even compared him to a vegetable.

Perhaps he's inched out into the garden, Sesame thought in terror. *Perhaps even now, something's eating him. He's such a lovely, chubby caterpillar. He'd be breakfast, lunch and supper for a blackbird . . .*

"Sesame!" Dame Fuddle said in despair. "Whatever is the matter with you today! You are usually such a graceful little fairy!"

Sesame stared at her feet. Bruised daisy petals were scattered all across the courtyard. "Sorry, Dame Fuddle," she said dully.

The last seed on the dandelion clock dropped off and spiralled into the sky. A sigh of relief rippled through the class. Fairy Deportment was over.

"Lunch!" said Tiptoe happily, as Dame Fuddle and the rest of the class hurried into the Dining Flowerpot.

"How can you think of food, Tiptoe?" Sesame demanded. "Sprout's gone missing! He could be in danger!"

Tiptoe blushed.

"He'll be sulking somewhere," Brilliance said.

"Sprout never goes anywhere without me!" Sesame insisted. "Even when he sulks, he does it round my feet."

They all stared around the courtyard. There was no place for a caterpillar to hide.

"Maybe he's in the dormitory?" Tiptoe suggested.

But apart from the sleeping ladybird, the fairies' dormitory was empty.

"Sprout might be at lunch already," said Nettle, as they headed down the dormitory corridor towards the Dining Flowerpot.

"Who knows?" said Kelpie. "Maybe he's saved us a table?"

"Don't joke about it!" Sesame begged. Tears were welling in her eyes again.

Ping patted her arm. "Trust me, Sesame. There's really nothing to worry about."

"How do you *know*?" Sesame wept.

"Because he's behind you," Ping said.

Sesame whirled around. Through her tears, she could see the blurry outline of a fat green caterpillar standing in the middle of the corridor.

"Sprout!" she choked out. "Sprout! I'm sorry!"

She scooped the caterpillar into her arms and hugged him. Then she tucked

him into the large pocket on the front of
her dress. Sprout curled up tight,
tucking his nose underneath his soft
green tummy.

"How cute," Tiptoe breathed.

"Totally adorable," Brilliance said, looking misty.

"It's just a caterpillar," said Kelpie. "Give me a bee any day."

Sprout didn't stir from Sesame's pocket during lunch. Sesame put a roasted daisy heart into her pocket for him to eat when he woke up, and vowed never to be horrible to her pet caterpillar again.

"I'm going to ask Lord Gallivant about borrowing a school butterfly for the Butterfly Cup," she said bravely, as they left the Dining Flowerpot. Flea zoomed around over their heads, happy to be back in the open air.

"That means we'll lose for sure," Nettle sighed.

"We'll lose anyway," Kelpie said, throwing honeycake crumbs in the air for Flea.

Sesame felt cross. "We might still win," she protested.

"If they let me enter Pong we would," Ping began.

"Not going to happen," Brilliance said firmly. "Look, Sesame. No one ever won the Butterfly Cup on a Cabbage White. And I heard Ambrosia Academy's got a Peacock this year."

The fairies gasped.

"Aren't Peacocks the fastest butterflies of all?" Nettle asked.

"Almost," Sesame admitted. "Brimstones are faster, but that's it."

Brilliance stopped. She smiled one of her brilliant smiles. "Naughty Fairies!" she said, and put out her hand.

"Nag fieldmice," said Nettle at once, putting her hand on top of Brilliance's. "What are you planning, Brilliance?"

Brilliance looked smug. "Not until everyone's done an NF. Kelpie?"

"Never fart," said Kelpie and plunked her hand on Nettle's.

"Knit frogspawn," said Sesame. "Euw,

34

Kelpie, your hands are filthy. Do I have to touch you?"

"Knit starts with a K," Brilliance said. "But it's OK just this once. Tiptoe?"

"Nasty flotsam," Tiptoe said after a moment, putting her hand on Sesame's.

"Nasturtium flavour!" said Ping rather grandly. She put her hand on Tiptoe's.

"Fly, fly, to the SKY!" the fairies chanted. On the word SKY, they all lifted their hands into the air.

"Right," Brilliance said, satisfied. "My plan is to go and spy on Ambrosia Academy and check out their butterflies for real."

The others gaped at Brilliance.

"That's against the rules," Tiptoe said at last.

"Exactly," said Brilliance. "That's why St Juniper's never wins. We never break the rules."

Kelpie looked offended. "We do break the rules," she said. "All the time."

"Not on the Butterfly Cup we don't,"
said Brilliance. "All that's about to
change. Sesame, that ladybird in the
dormitory looked OK to me. Is it ready
to go back outside?"

Sesame nodded. "We can probably
release it later this afternoon."

"The Sports Field is a dangerous place for a ladybird," Brilliance said. "I think the Meadow would be much safer. Don't you?"

"The Ambrosia Academy fairies will be butterfly riding in the Meadow this evening," Tiptoe said.

Brilliance smiled. "Exactly."

After supper, Sesame, Brilliance, Nettle, Kelpie and Tiptoe gathered in the dormitory. The ladybird was now wide awake. As Sesame gave it a pat, it opened its wing cases and stretched its gauzy wings.

"Save it for the Meadow, little guy," said Tiptoe.

Sesame carefully peeled the bandage off the ladybird's leg. Sprout muttered from deep inside Sesame's pocket as Nettle tucked the ladybird under her arm. Brilliance and Sesame checked out of the window. Four

grumpy-looking fairies were on detention, slowly sweeping leaves and twigs out of the courtyard with grass brooms. Dame Lacewing, St Juniper's scary Fairy Maths teacher, was taking the detention. Sesame's heart gave a little flutter. If Dame Lacewing spotted them leaving the school grounds without permission, they'd be in big trouble.

"Hurry up, Ping," Brilliance muttered, looking up at the sky.

Ping suddenly swept over the courtyard on Pong. The wind from Pong's wings sent the swept leaves and twigs scootling back into the courtyard. Looking furious, the detention fairies threw their grass brooms to the ground and muttered darkly at each other, and Dame Lacewing marched over to the nearest fairy to tell her off.

"Now!" Brilliance hissed, and jumped out of the dormitory window. Nettle followed, holding the ladybird tight. Sesame tucked Sprout as far down in her pocket as she could, and followed Nettle. Tiptoe was next. Kelpie was last, sitting lightly on Flea's back and digging her heels into the bumblebee's furry sides.

Sesame had never flown so fast in her life. They darted over the courtyard, and out of sight behind the flowerpots. Sesame put her head down and zoomed into the tunnel through the Hedge, following the others.

The Meadow's grassy wilderness spread below them like a carpet. On the far side of the Meadow was the Wood. Sesame squinted through the trees. She could see the toadstool towers of Ambrosia Academy nestled in the roots of a large oak tree near the edge of the Wood.

"Right," Brilliance panted, as they touched down as close to the Wood as they dared. "If anyone sees us, we're returning the ladybird to its natural habitat, OK. We aren't checking out the opposition."

"And we're not sneaking a look at the Ambrosia butterflies either," Tiptoe nodded.

"Well, well, well," came a triumphant voice nearby. "If it isn't a bunch of sneaky little Juniper spies."

4

Ambrosia Academy

St Juniper's and Ambrosia Academy
were deadly enemies. St Juniper's
hated Ambrosia Academy because they
thought they were so much better than
St Juniper's, with their pretty rose-petal
uniforms and their rich and important
families. Ambrosia Academy hated St
Juniper's because their school was
made of broken flowerpots instead of
beautiful toadstools. The two schools
had hated each other for as long as
anyone could remember – and at
Butterfly Cup time, they always hated
each other even more. This was
especially true this year, as the prize
was a school trip to a famous

greenhouse, where the fairies could swim in warm ponds and sunbathe on leaves and make clothes from exotic flowers like orchids and lilies. The scruffily dressed St Juniper's fairies dreamed of dresses made of orchids, and even rich fairies loved lilies.

Three Ambrosia Academy fairies stood high on a leaf. They wore beautiful dresses of pale pink rose petals. Their noses were cute and their cheeks were rosy. They all had blonde ringlets. Sesame had a nasty feeling that their breath smelled of lavender.

"That's *Saint* Juniper's to you, Globber," Kelpie snarled, sliding off Flea and holding up her fists.

"And that's *Glitter*, not *Globber*, you smelly little *spy*," said the tallest, blondest, prettiest Ambrosia Academy fairy. "Wait till I tell Lady Campion about this."

Nettle put the ladybird down on the

grass. "We're here on school business," she said. The ladybird chittered something and rushed into the undergrowth. "This ladybird was sick and now it's better, so we're returning it to the wild. Tell your head teacher *that*."

Glitter looked smug. "I'll tell her what I like," she said. "And you'll back me up, won't you, Glee?" She turned to the tiny fairy on her right.

"Of courth!" squeaked the tiny fairy. Sesame noticed she had a very fat ladybird tucked under her arm.

"Gloss?"

"Like you had to ask," drawled the fairy on Glitter's left. She adjusted the pair of butterfly reins in her hand. Sesame followed the reins up into the sky, half excited, half dreading what she would see.

Hovering above the Ambrosia Academy fairies was a fantastic Peacock butterfly. Its wings were bright red, with

two large spots of purple, black and
yellow on each wing. It looked strong
and fast and . . .

"Gorgeous," Sesame breathed. It was
the most beautiful butterfly she had
ever seen.

Gloss glanced at Sesame. "Look while
you can," she sneered. "You won't get a
chance in the Butterfly Cup, because

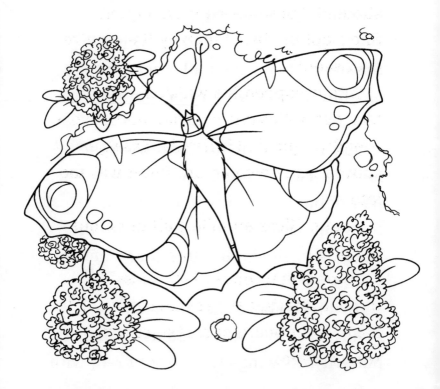

Splendid will be going too fast."

"That's all you know," Tiptoe said. "We've got good butterflies too."

Glitter raised one eyebrow. "Reeeeeally?" she purred.

"Leave it," Sesame muttered, tugging at Tiptoe's arm.

Tiptoe shook off Sesame's hand.

"We're going to win this year!" she shouted. "Sesame's our champion. She's got the best butterfly that you've ever seen!"

Sprout popped his whiskery green face out of Sesame's pocket and gave a friendly squeak. Hurriedly, Sesame shoved him down again. But it was too late.

Glitter, Gloss and Glee all burst out laughing.

"*That* is your butterfly?" Gloss giggled, staring at Sesame's pocket. "I have never heard of slugs getting wings before."

"It'th thtill a caterpillar!" Glee trilled.

"Ooh, ooh, ooh," Glitter held on to her sides. "I'm going to burst out of my dress."

Glee stopped laughing. "Don't," she said. "That'th like a totally fantathtic dreth."

"Take my advice," Glitter said, wiping her eyes. "Don't bother turning up to the race. You'll only embarrass yourselves. We're going to win the Butterfly Cup for Ambrosia Academy, like we do every year. Go and tell fuddy-duddy Fuddle that!"

"Besides," Gloss added, "dresses made of orchids are hardly St Juniper's style, are they? They really wouldn't suit your little flowerpot lives."

Still laughing, the Ambrosia Academy fairies jumped off the leaf and flew away. Sesame watched Gloss riding low on Splendid's back until they were just a tiny speck in the distance.

"That didn't go as well as I'd hoped," said Brilliance after a moment.

"Nope," Nettle said.

"I enjoyed it," said Kelpie, putting down her fists.

"Sorry," Tiptoe said, looking sheepish. "That was my fault. But those Ambrosia Academy fairies make me so mad . . ."

"Don't worry about it, Tiptoe," Sesame said. Somewhere in her head, a small idea was starting to form.

"We *have* to win now!" Brilliance declared. "I'm going to get an orchid dress if it kills me."

"I will speak to Lord Gallivant," said Ping, as they took off and headed back to the Hedge. "I will make him change the rules and let me fly Pong."

"Shut up, Ping," said Kelpie, from Flea's back. "You're not helping."

The small idea in Sesame's head grew bigger as they flew through the dark Hedge Tunnel. By the time they could see the flowerpot towers of St Juniper's, the small idea had grown bigger. When the highest flowerpot tower came into view . . .

"Naughty Fairies!" Sesame gasped as soon as they touched down on the highest flowerpot tower.

"Need flatulence," said Kelpie, dismounting from Flea.

"Nose flap," Tiptoe suggested.

"Neigh fruitily," Nettle said.

Ping gave a nasty smile. "Nibble phlegm."

"Urgh," Sesame shuddered. "That's the grossest one ever."

"And phlegm starts with a 'p'," said Brilliance, "but who cares? Noxious fumes."

"Fly, fly, to the SKY!" the fairies chanted, and flung their hands up into the air.

Everyone looked at Sesame.

"Tell," Brilliance ordered.

"Does anyone know a transforming spell?" Sesame asked hopefully.

"I can turn a spoon into a dragon," Ping said. Ping had performed this trick during her first week at St Juniper's.

"Can you turn a caterpillar into a butterfly?" Sesame asked.

"You don't need a spell for that," Nettle said. "They do it anyway."

Sesame pulled Sprout out of her pocket and held him up in the air for everyone to see. "But Sprout's *not* doing it, is he?" she said. "We need to speed things up. How does your transforming spell work, Ping?"

"You sprinkle dragon-tree sap on to the thing you want to change, and say a magic word," Ping said. "It's easy. I'll do it now if you like."

"Won't dragon-tree sap turn Sprout into a dragon?" Sesame asked cautiously, tucking Sprout back into her

pocket. Sprout grunted and settled back
to sleep.

"Maybe!" Ping said. She sounded
enthusiastic.

Brilliance smiled one of her most
brilliant smiles. "If dragon-tree sap
makes dragons," she said, "butterfly
powder will make butterflies."

"Depends on what kind of butterfly
Sprout's going to turn into," Nettle
said, swinging one of her ear spiders

around on her finger. "You'll need the right kind of powder, or weird things might happen."

Everyone looked at Sesame.

"Sprout's a Cabbage White, I think," Sesame said, looking down at the top of Sprout's bright green head.

"Bor-ing," Kelpie sighed, and went back to untangling a knot in Flea's fur.

"Some Cabbage Whites are faster than others," Sesame said with dignity. "I think Sprout's going to be a Small White."

"Is that good?" Ping asked.

"Kind of," Sesame said bravely.

"Tiptoe, fly down to the stables and get some Cabbage White powder," Brilliance ordered. "Let's not do the spell up here. It's too exposed. We'll do it in the Strawberry Patch."

Brilliance, Nettle, Sesame, Kelpie and Ping flew to the Strawberry Patch to wait for Tiptoe. Five dandelion seeds later, Tiptoe swooped back into view.

"Lord Gallivant nearly saw me," Tiptoe panted, giving the pot of butterfly powder to Brilliance. "But something distracted him."

"Probably his reflection," said Kelpie.

Sesame carefully lifted Sprout out of her pocket and put him down on the ground. She kissed him quickly, and stepped back behind Nettle. She didn't want to watch the spell.

Brilliance handed the butterfly powder to Ping. Ping took a pinch and sprinkled it on Sprout, who sneezed.

"*Mudario*!" Ping shouted. She raised her hands dramatically, and knocked a ripe strawberry off an overhead stem.

"Whoops," Kelpie said. "Messy. You shouldn't have done the handwaving thing. There was no handwaving when you turned that spoon into a dragon."

"Stop talking and help!" Nettle said, rushing over to Ping. The others

followed. Flea zoomed in to lick some strawberry juice off Ping's cheeks.

"English strawberries grow too low," said Ping in a dignified voice.

Sesame suddenly remembered Sprout. She turned and looked at her caterpillar. Her heart lurched. "Guys?" she whispered. "Problem."

"We know," Brilliance said, dabbing at Ping's shoulders. "Strawberry juice leaves awful stains."

"No!" Sesame wailed. "We've turned Sprout into an earthworm!"

5

Wormy Blues

A long brown earthworm lay on the ground in front of the fairies.

Brilliance frowned. "That's not a butterfly."

"Give brainbox here a honeycake," Kelpie said. Flea looked hopeful at the mention of honeycakes.

Sesame burst into tears, and ran to Sprout. She flung her arms around his thick brown neck. "Sprout, oh Sprout!" she sobbed.

"I think that's his bum," Nettle said.

Sesame sobbed louder and rushed to Sprout's other end.

"He looks cute as a worm," Tiptoe said, putting her arm around Sesame.

"A worm in the Butterfly Cup," said Kelpie. "This I have to see."

"Shut up, Kelpie!" Tiptoe, Ping, Nettle and Brilliance chorused.

"The butterfly powder must have had earthworm poo in it," Sesame wept. There was a smear of earthworm slime on her cheek.

"Euw," Brilliance said.

The new, wormy Sprout raised his slender neck and sniffed the air. Then he began to wiggle away from the fairies, towards a patch of soft earth. Nettle jumped on his back. "Oh no, you don't!" she said. "We're not losing you now!"

Brilliance grabbed Sprout's tail. Tiptoe clung on behind Nettle. Sesame laid her cheek on what she hoped was Sprout's neck and cried some more. Kelpie got some silk from Nettle's ear spiders and made a pair of reins, which Ping fitted carefully around Sprout's head end.

"Try pulling," Ping said, handing the reins to Sesame. The other fairies climbed off Sprout's back.

Sesame got to her feet and tugged on the reins. Sprout's head swung around in her direction. After a moment, he moved his slim brown body across the ground towards her.

"He still recognises me," she said with relief.

Sprout's head stretched and sniffed around Sesame's skirt.

"He can smell strawberry juice on you," Kelpie said. "That stuff drives Flea wild."

The fairies straggled out of the Strawberry Patch towards the school courtyard. After making sure that no teachers were on duty, they tugged Sprout towards the dormitory. He was so long that his tail was still in the courtyard while his head was sliding under Sesame's bed. He sniffed at the strawberry juice on Sesame's shoes.

"Now I don't even have a caterpillar, let alone a butterfly," Sesame muttered, as Sprout curled the rest of his body underneath her bed.

"We can reverse this worm thing," said Brilliance confidently. "I know a spell—"

"No more spells," Kelpie said, ducking underneath a thick brown leaf which was hanging from the flowerpot ceiling and plunking herself down on

her bed. "We'll end up turning Sprout
into something much worse. No. We
have to get creative if we have any
chance of winning the Butterfly Cup
this year."

Nettle sat up straight. "A wild
butterfly hunt!" she said. "I'll get my
spiders to make some lassos. We've got
two weeks. If we can't catch a butterfly
by then, we don't deserve to win the
Cup. I mean, how hard can it be?"

All week, Sesame's dreams were full of butterflies. They flew over her head, swooping around her on colourful wings. A Painted Lady, a Comma, a Brimstone, even. But however hard she jumped and flew and whirled her lasso, the butterflies always slipped away.

How hard can it be? How hard can it be? Nettle's words mocked Sesame every morning and every evening. Butterfly catching wasn't as easy as Nettle had predicted. The butterflies flittered up and down and sideways, and always settled on a different flower to the one the fairies thought they'd settle on.

"It's like they're laughing at us," Sesame said through gritted teeth, as she untangled her lasso from another empty flower on the Buddleia Bush. The butterflies loved the bright purple buddleia flowers, and the air was thick with butterfly wings.

"Butterflies never laugh," said Tiptoe. "It knocks the powder off their wings and then they can't fly."

"Talking of flying," said Brilliance, zooming past as she chased a ragged-winged Tortoiseshell, "isn't it the first Butterfly Cup practice tonight?"

"It's stupid, only being allowed to start practising one week before the race," Kelpie grumbled. "I bet Ambrosia Academy's been practising already."

"What time is it?" Sesame gasped.

"Twenty-five past the dandelion," said Nettle. She stared in disgust at the bluebottle struggling in her lasso. "You've got five dandelion seeds to get to the Butterfly Stables, or Lord Gallivant might kick you off the team."

"Ask him about the Midsummer Champion Butterfly Race and he might lend you Plankton!" Kelpie called, as Sesame dropped her lasso and flew off in a panic.

*

Lord Gallivant tutted as Sesame streaked down to the Butterfly Stable panting and out of breath. "You are late, young fairy," he said severely, sitting astride his magnificent Red Admiral butterfly Plankton. "When I won the Midsummer Champion Butterfly Race, timing was everything. Where is your butterfly?"

Sesame flushed. "I don't have one yet," she whispered miserably. "I'm trying to catch one, Lord Gallivant," she added in a rush, "I'm going to get a really good one, it's just – there's been a bit of a delay, and . . ."

The three other fairies on the St Juniper's Butterfly Cup team started whispering.

"Silence," Lord Gallivant thundered. "What did you say, Onion?"

"Do you want silence, or do you want me to tell you what I said, sir?" asked Onion, a thin fairy on an even thinner

Large White. The pink-haired fairy on the Small White giggled.

"Stop laughing, Vetch!" Lord Gallivant shouted. "And don't be cheeky, Onion!"

"Onion said Sesame shouldn't be on the team," piped up Pelly, a fat fairy with pompoms of blonde hair, who was sitting on an even fatter Meadow Brown.

"You sneak, *Pelargonium*!" Onion shot back. Vetch giggled again.

Pelly leaped off the Meadow Brown with her fists flailing. Onion fell off her Large White with a thump.

"Stop it this instant, or you shall *all* be off the team!" Lord Gallivant roared. "Don't you want to swim in warm pools and sunbathe on enormous shiny leaves and make gorgeous outfits out of orchid petals? *I* certainly do." He looked a bit dreamy. "We have to work together!"

Sesame peered hopefully into the

darkness of the Butterfly Stables. There
were a few decent school Whites. Just
as long as she didn't have to ride—

"You'll have to take Snowball,
Sesame," Lord Gallivant announced.
"We can't delay any longer. Pelar . . ."

The fat fairy glared.

"Pelly," said Lord Gallivant hurriedly.

"You shall ride first, then Onion, then Vetch, with Sesame bringing up the rear. Remember Sesame – as the last fairy, you must make one extra run to the finish. To your starting positions!"

Sesame slowly mounted Snowball. Snowball was the biggest, most ragged butterfly in the St Juniper's stables. His wings were almost see-through with age, and his furry head was going bald.

At Lord Gallivant's signal, Pelly crouched down over her Meadow Brown, Syrup, and streaked across the Sports Field, as far as the cobweb trampoline and back again.

"Pelargonium," Onion crooned, then zoomed off on her Large White, Stinker, before Pelly could hit her.

Zoomed was the wrong word, Sesame decided, watching Onion urging Stinker towards the trampoline. Stinker swayed and wobbled from side to side, sinking lower and lower until Onion's feet were almost trailing the ground.

"Stay in the air!" Lord Gallivant shouted, flying above Onion. "If your feet touch the ground in the Butterfly Cup, you'll be disqualified!"

Somehow, Onion stayed in the air, turned Stinker around and lumbered back to the Butterfly Stables. Vetch wasn't much better. Her butterfly Gruesome kept veering to the left, as if he had one wing bigger than the other.

"Gruesome's got one wing bigger than the other," Vetch explained, as she returned to the Butterfly Stables.

"Pull him to the right next time," said Lord Gallivant. "Off you go, Sesame!"

Sesame kicked Snowball. Snowball rose off the ground, then sank again.

Before she could do anything about it, Sesame's feet had landed on the springy grass.

"You're out, you're out, you're out" Onion chanted.

"Never mind, Sesame," said Lord Gallivant briskly. "When I won the

Midsummer Champion Butterfly Race, I
didn't have a butterfly until the last
dandelion seed." He patted her on the
shoulder. "Back here at the same time
tomorrow, young fairies! We just need to
practise, practise, practise!"

With a heavy heart, Sesame put
Snowball back in the stables and gave
him some nectar. Then she dusted his
frail wings with butterfly powder. "No
offence, Snowball," she said, resting her
head against his balding cheek, "but
I'm not going to ride you at the
Butterfly Cup." Snowball gave a croaky
butterfly purr. "I've decided to resign

from the team," Sesame whispered. A
tear rolled down her cheek. "I'll tell
Lord Gallivant in the morning."

6

Nerves

It was dark by the time Sesame got back to the dormitory.

"Where have you been?" Brilliance demanded, sitting up in bed. "Onion told us that practice finished ages ago. Dame Lacewing's been round twice, asking for you."

"What did you tell her?" Sesame felt anxious.

"We said you had the runs," Nettle said. "Butterfly Cup nerves."

"She left pretty quickly after that," Kelpie said, yawning.

"So, where *have* you been?" Brilliance repeated.

"Thinking," Sesame said. "Did you

catch anything after I went to practice?"

"A bluebottle, a damselfly, thirty-three buddleia flowers and a cricket," Tiptoe said gloomily.

"So, how did the practice go?" Brilliance asked.

Sesame bent down and stroked Sprout, whose long, wormy shape was curled up under the bed. "I've made a decision," she said. "I'm not going to fly in the Butterfly Cup. I'm going to give my place to someone else."

"But you're St Juniper's best rider!" Nettle gasped. "We don't stand a chance if you resign!"

"We don't stand a chance anyway," Kelpie muttered.

"Why are you always so negative, Kelpie?" Tiptoe said crossly.

Kelpie shrugged. "Saves disappointment. Ouch!" Rubbing her head, she stared at the thick brown leaf that was still hanging over her bed. "I wish Dame Lacewing would get some detention fairies to come and do some sweeping up here," she muttered, before sticking her head under her pillow. Flea gave a sleepy buzz from the windowsill.

"I could ride Pong," Ping began.

Brilliance cut her off. "Don't resign, Sesame," she said fiercely. "We'll find you a butterfly. Please, don't go to Lord Gallivant!"

"But Snowball was a disaster!" Sesame wailed. "He hardly got off the ground!"

"Lord Gallivant made you ride *Snowball*?" Tiptoe asked. "Does he *want* us to lose?"

"Lord Gallivant won't ask you to ride Snowball in the Butterfly Cup," Ping said with confidence.

"That's easy for you to say," Sesame said glumly.

Ping shrugged. "I saw him this

evening, when I checked on Pong. He's put three of the school butterflies on a rest-and-relax programme in the back of the Butterfly Stables. Nectar and gentle flapping three times a day. I expect he'll put you on one of those tomorrow."

Sesame felt a little more hopeful. If she didn't have to ride Snowball, she might fly a decent race after all.

"Can we go to sleep now?" Kelpie demanded.

Sesame trailed her hand over her bed and stroked Sprout's cool, slippery neck. "Sorry," she said. "Course you can, Kelpie. Night, everyone."

The second Butterfly Cup practice was worse than the first.

"Try Salt today, Sesame," Lord Gallivant advised, handing the Large White's reins to Sesame. "He's had some extra rations overnight. Should fly like an arrow." He glanced around. "Where's Pelly?"

"Detention, Lord Gallivant," Vetch said. "Dame Fuddle called her Pelargonium in Fairy Deportment."

Lord Gallivant made an effort to control his temper. "I shall ride the first part today," he said. "Then we shall go as before." He dug his legs into Plankton's sides.

"I don't think Plankton's going to turn in time," said Sesame anxiously. Lord Gallivant was struggling to avoid the cobweb trampoline.

"That'll be the snail slime I put on his reins," Onion said as a red-faced Lord Gallivant limped back to the starting line. She kicked her Large White. "Come on, Stinker! Let's show 'em!"

Stinker lumbered as far as the cobweb trampoline, but got distracted by a nearby buddleia bush. Lord Gallivant was almost as purple as the buddleia

flowers by the time Onion made it back
to the starting line. Vetch started well,
but pulled Gruesome so far to the right
that she crashed into the ivy-covered
fence. Sesame made it to the cobweb
trampoline and back again. As she
made the turn to race back to the

cobweb trampoline one last time, Lord
Gallivant burst into tears.

"It's no use, Sesame! It's over!" he
shouted. "Well and truly over!"

"The practice?" Onion asked him
hopefully.

"My career!" Lord Gallivant howled.

Butterfly Cup day dawned bright and clear. The flowerpot towers of St Juniper's were fluttering with petal pennants, and there was an air of festivity in the corridors.

"Eat up," Tiptoe urged Sesame as she poked at the forget-me-not pastry on her plate. "You need your energy today."

The teachers filed past the table to wish Sesame good luck. Sesame could hardly hear them for the nervous drumming in her ears.

"Keep low on the butterfly's back," Dame Lacewing advised. "You're the last one in the race – make it count."

"Keep your wings tightly folded." This was Dame Honey, the Fairy English teacher. "That way you'll fly more smoothly."

"Pelly's been improving this week," Brilliance said encouragingly as they headed for the Assembly Flowerpot,

where Dame Fuddle would give the traditional Butterfly Cup Address. "That Meadow Brown of hers, Syrup – I think he's lost weight. Onion and Vetch aren't up to much, but you'll make up the time. Who are you riding, anyway?"

"Ivory," Sesame whispered.

"You said yourself that you've never known Ivory in such good condition," Tiptoe said, tucking her arm through Sesame's elbow.

"I know what I said." Sesame's teeth were chattering with nerves. "But . . ."

"But nothing," Kelpie said smartly. "You'll be fine. We'll get the best seats and cheer you the whole way. Ping's going to fly us to the Meadow on Pong, so we'll get there miles before anyone else—"

Sesame could hear her heartbeat roaring in her ears. She stared at her friends. "I can't do this," she said dumbly. "I'm sorry – I can't . . ." And she turned around and ran out of the St Juniper's courtyard.

Sesame kept running until she was deep in the Nettle Patch. Then she threw herself to the ground and cried. She'd let down the team. She'd let down St Juniper's. She'd let down her friends. She had no caterpillar, no butterfly, no pride, nothing.

After almost half a dandelion, Sesame got to her feet. Wearily, she unfurled her wings and flew back to St Juniper's. The school was deserted. The dandelion clock in the middle of the courtyard showed eight dandelion seeds until the start of the race. The whole school had gone to the Meadow to watch. Sesame trudged into the Dormitory Flowerpot. She'd start packing immediately. That way, she'd be long gone by the time everyone got back.

The earthworm was stretched full length on Sesame's bed, his slim head resting on the pillow. Sesame reached out to stroke him. "I can't take you with me, Sprout," she whispered sadly. "You'll be better here."

A crackling noise on the ceiling made her turn her head. She stared. The thick brown leaf over Kelpie's bed was wriggling.

Sesame felt her knees give way. It wasn't a leaf. It was a *chrysalis*.

A butterfly wriggled out and landed with a plop on the floor. Its wings were crumpled and greenish. Sesame had a strange feeling that she'd seen it somewhere before.

The butterfly raised its head and blinked at Sesame. It squeaked.

"Sprout?" Sesame said faintly. "Is that you?"

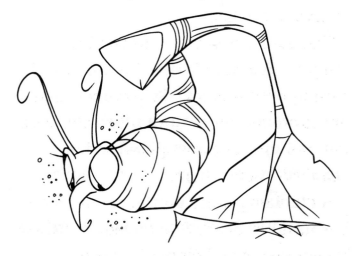

The butterfly squeaked again. It straightened its wings a little more. Then it opened them. Sesame was dazzled by the bright yellow colour which flooded the room.

"Sprout!" Sesame whispered. "You're . . . you're a *Brimstone*?"

7

The Race

The gorgeous Brimstone butterfly stood
proudly in front of Sesame.

"I don't understand," Sesame
stammered. "Isn't the earthworm –
you?"

The butterfly turned his regal head
and stared at the earthworm on
Sesame's bed. He gave a jealous growl.
And Sesame knew.

She flung her arms around the
butterfly's neck. "You did it!" she wept,
raining kisses on Sprout's furry head.
Sprout started purring as Sesame's
mind whirled with dizzy, glittering joy.
It was a mistake! It had all been a
mistake! Sprout must have started

pupating the day that he went missing
– the caterpillar they found in the
corridor was a different caterpillar all
together – and the earthworm . . .
Sesame couldn't take it in.

Sprout butted gently at her arm.

"I can't call you Sprout any more,"
Sesame said joyfully, brushing the tears
from her eyes. "You're much too
beautiful. I'll call you Sulphur. Strong,
bright, yellow – *and mine!*"

And she leapt nimbly on Sulphur's
back and flew straight out of the
dormitory window, soaring up and away
– over the school, and over the Hedge,
and down to the Meadow, where the
Butterfly Cup was about to start.

Rows of fairies sat on either side of the
racecourse, which cut through the long
grass of the Meadow. St Juniper's flags
waved on one side, and Ambrosia
Academy flags on the other. There was

a band of pixie musicians playing grass harps, and stalls selling butterfly powders, clover buns, petal bunting and magic wands which claimed: "WAVE IT AND WIN!" At the far end was the finishing line – the Wood Stump itself.

Sesame swooped casually over the racecourse and landed next to Lord Gallivant.

"Where have you been?" Lord Gallivant grabbed Sesame's arm. "And what – what . . ."

"This is Sulphur," Sesame said, almost choking with pride. "I told you I'd get a butterfly, Lord Gallivant."

"My dear child!" Lord Gallivant cried. "A Brimstone! Do you know what this means?"

"We can put Onion on Ivory?" Sesame suggested as she dug her heels into Sulphur's sides. Sulphur shot into the air like a streak of gold.

A voice crackled through the Meadow. "To your starting positions!"

The two teams were waiting at the starting line.

"Onion!" Sesame yelled, as the St Juniper's team stared up at her in amazement. "Leave Stinker and take Ivory, quickly!"

Glitter was leading the Ambrosia Academy team on her nervy-looking Tortoiseshell butterfly. There were two other Ambrosia Academy fairies Sesame didn't recognise, both riding Painted

Ladies. Gloss, sitting astride Splendid, stared in horror as Sesame flew down and landed lightly beside her.

"Scared yet?" Sesame asked casually. "You should be."

The fairies in the crowd were chanting, "Start! Start! Start!"

Glitter turned to Pelly. Her eyes gleamed with malice. "Pelargonium, isn't it?" she purred.

There was a crack as Dame Campion, Head of Ambrosia Academy, broke the starting twig.

"I'll get you!" Pelly roared in fury, digging her heels into Syrup as Glitter streaked away. Sesame had never seen Pelly fly so fast.

"You've got a Brimstone!" Onion grinned at Sesame in wonder. "We're bound to win the greenhouse trip now!"

Onion bent low over Ivory's back as Pelly and Glitter raced across the line. She didn't look round as Pelly jumped

off her butterfly and started hitting
Glitter.

"Go! Go! Go!" roared the watching
fairies. Sesame stared down the
racecourse, looking for the others. She
spotted Pong and Flea, both hovering
by the Wood Stump. Her friends were
sitting just below them, next to the
finishing line. They hadn't seen her yet.

Onion scorched over the line, beating
the Ambrosia fairy by a whisker. Pelly
was still hitting Glitter as Vetch gave a

yell and drove her butterfly Gruesome forward.

"Right!" Sesame screamed, waving her arms. "Pull him right! Now left!"

Gruesome swung left and right and left again, wasting precious time. Ambrosia Academy's second Painted Lady butterfly overtook with ease, flying smoothly to the Wood Stump and back again.

"See you later," Gloss sneered, as the Painted Lady rocketed back over the line. Splendid flapped his magnificent wings, and he and Gloss were off in a heartbeat.

"Sorry!" Vetch was almost in tears, hauling hard at Gruesome's reins half a dandelion seed later. "I've ruined everything!"

"No time to talk!" Sesame yelled. She dug her heels into Sulphur's sides, and the racecourse became a blur.

Sesame was aware of cheering fairies,

and blue sky over her head, and the
strong beat of Sulphur's wings
brushing her knees. The Wood Stump
grew nearer and nearer. She met Gloss
already heading back to the starting
line, who smirked and waved at her.

Cold purpose set like a stone in
Sesame's heart. At the Wood Stump,
she pulled Sulphur into a squealing
turn. There was just time to see her
friends' astonished faces below her,
before she was speeding back to the
starting line as well.

The crowd gasped as Flea's stupid

face loomed in front of Sesame. The
bumblebee had flown into the middle of
the racecourse for a better view.

"Out of the way, Flea!" Sesame
yelled, pulling hard at Sulphur's reins.
Sulphur shot straight up in the air, then
down again as the crowd oohed.

Gloss had reached the starting line.
Now she was turning, ready to make
the final dash for the Wood Stump. The
crowd was roaring itself hoarse as
Sesame urged Sulphur on.

"No chance," Gloss sneered, racing
past Sesame.

But Splendid had flown too close to Sulphur. The two butterflies spun away from each other, caught up in brightly coloured tailspins. Sesame was the first to recover, driving Sulphur out of his spin and across the starting line. As Sesame made the turn and headed for the Wood Stump one last time, Splendid was still spinning down, down, down – until Gloss's feet were touching the grass.

"Out!" screamed the St Juniper's fairies. The stands erupted as Sesame and Sulphur streaked down the cheering racecourse, past the throngs of yelling supporters, the fluttering banners – and across the line at the base of the Wood Stump.

St Juniper's had won the Butterfly Cup.

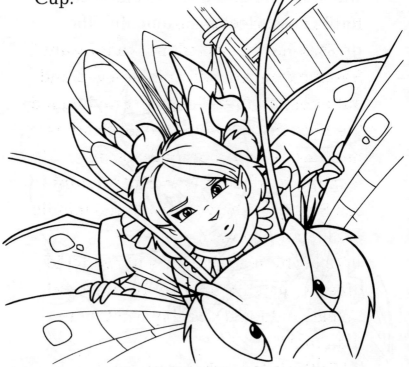

Half of St Juniper's wanted to carry Sesame and Sulphur back to school on their shoulders. The other half argued that it would take them days to get across the Meadow that way, and wouldn't it be much better to fly and celebrate back at school with Turnip the kitchen pixie's famous garlic puff pie, which he had promised to make in honour of the occasion.

"They haven't asked me what *I* want," Sesame grinned, still sparkle-eyed and out of breath from the race. She hugged the Butterfly Cup close to her heart as her friends jostled around her, all wanting to touch it. She could hardly see Sulphur, who was lost in the middle of an adoring crowd.

"Apart from a fabulous yellow orchid dress to match Sulphur?" Nettle joked. "What could you possibly want more than that?"

"Glitter's face when you won,"

Brilliance said. "In a frame."

"Garlic puff pie," said Tiptoe
dreamily.

"I want to know if that caterpillar
really did change into an earthworm,"
Sesame said. "Or if the earthworm just
turned up when we weren't looking."
She handed the cup to Onion, who
screamed with delight and held it in the
air.

"The spell was a duff," Kelpie said.
She glared at Flea, who was standing
sheepishly next to her. "Like certain

bees I could mention."

Flea buzzed an apology.

"My spell was *not* a duff," Ping said indignantly.

"I guess we'll never know," Sesame said. She put her arms around as many of her friends as she could reach. "But who cares? We've got a greenhouse to go to!"

Imps are Wimps

Fairy Science is just NOT cool.

So when the Naughty Fairies face a science test they need some magic help.

But what do imps and creepy crawlies have to do with it?

It's all part of Brilliance's brilliant plan . . .